The Nervous Turtle

Authored by Brody Krusemark and Sean Krusemark

Illustrated by ScribeBright Press

Published by ScribeBright Press, Emerson, NE 68733
ISBN: 978-0692331552
Story created and authored by Brody Krusemark and Sean Krusemark
Edited and illustrated by ScribeBright Press
ScribeBright Press is a registered trade name in the state of Nebraska
This edition first printed, 2015
scribebright.com

In the Deep, Deep Forest lived a very nervous turtle.

In fact, he was so nervous that he

never

ever

EVER

came out of his shell.

One day, Crocodile saw The Nervous Turtle. He tried **snarling loudly** at Turtle to get him out of his shell.

SNARL!

But The Nervous Turtle still

STILL

did not

come out of his shell.

Then Bear came.
"What are you doing, Crocodile?" Bear asked.

Crocodile said, "Trying to get Turtle out of his shell."

Just then Beaver came.

Bear and Crocodile asked
Beaver for help.

"You can chop down a tree and make a loud noise with us."

Rabbit heard the loud sounds and came
to see what was happening.

"What is going on?"
asked Rabbit.

Bear said, "We are trying to get Turtle out of his shell."

"Can you help us?" asked Beaver. "You can make a loud noise with your feet."

But The Nervous Turtle did not come out of his shell.

Just then Little Bird flew by.
"What are you doing?" she asked.

"Can I help you?" asked Little Bird.

"No," said Rabbit.

"You are too tiny," exclaimed Beaver.

"You cannot help us," stated Bear.

"You cannot make a loud noise," remarked Crocodile.

"But I do not need to make a loud noise," Little Bird said.

"Turtle, would you **please** come out and play with us?" Little Bird asked.

Then The Nervous Turtle...

slowly came out of his shell.

"Ok," said Turtle.

"Let's go play."

Thanks for reading.

Made in the USA
San Bernardino, CA
02 April 2015